D0241734

This edition produced for
THE BOOK PEOPLE LTD
Hall Wood Avenue, Haydock,
St Helens WA11 9UL,
by LITTLE TIGER PRESS
An imprint of Magi Publications
1 The Coda Centre, 189 Munster Road,
London SW6 6AW
www.littletigerpress.com

Originally published in Germany 2002
by Baumhaus Verlag, Frankfurt
First published in Great Britain 2003
Text and illustrations © Klaus Baumgart 2002
English text © Little Tiger Press 2003

All rights reserved • ISBN 1 85430 955 2

Printed in Singapore by Tien Wah Press Pte.

2 4 6 8 10 9 7 5 3

Jennifer

Laura's Secret

Klaus Baumgart

English text by Judy Waite

TED SMART

It was a wild night. The wind battered the house.
Laura and her little brother Tommy couldn't sleep.
"I've just had a brilliant idea," said Laura, watching the leaves swirl past the window. "Let's make a kite."
Mum and Dad thought it was a brilliant idea too.
They cut and they stuck. They trimmed and they tied.
"Can we fly it now?" asked Tommy excitedly.
"It's too late tonight," said Mum.
"And too dark," added Laura. "We wouldn't be able to see it. Kites don't shine like stars."

Laura knew a lot about stars. She had a special star. A secret star. She talked to it every night.

Later that night Laura told her star all about the wonderful new kite.

Suddenly Tommy rushed into her room.
"Could our kite fly as high as the stars?" he said.
"It would need to be amazing to fly that far," smiled Laura. "But sometimes, if you believe in something and you wish hard enough, you can help make it happen."
Out in the darkness Laura's star twinkled and shone.

The next day Laura and Tommy went to the park early.
"This is going to be brilliant," said Tommy.
"Just look at those other kites," said Laura. "They're really going high."
Suddenly Tommy looked nervous. "That's Joe West and his friends from school. They're always horrible to me."
"Well they won't be horrible today," said Laura firmly. "Not when they see how high our kite can fly."

But the kite didn't fly high. Laura and Tommy tried their best, but the kite kept drifting down on to the ground.

"That kite's just an old scrap of paper!" Joe shouted.

"Rubbish kite. Rubbish kite," sang one of his friends.

"Stick it in the bin!" yelled the other.

Determined, Tommy ran faster. Suddenly Joe stuck out his foot. Tommy tripped and tumbled to the ground. There was a terrible ripping sound.

"Oh no!" Tommy looked at his kite and his eyes filled with tears. "I've ripped it."

Joe and his friends started laughing, "Ha ha, your rubbish kite really can go in the bin now," and they laughed even louder.

Laura and Tommy carried the kite back through the windy park.

"Joe is right," said Tommy sadly. "It is only paper. It will never fly as high as the stars."

Laura hugged Tommy. She hated seeing him so sad. She hated seeing him being bullied. She didn't say anything, but her mind was spinning a secret plan.

That night Laura gazed up into the sky again.
Dark clouds rolled by.
There were no stars to be seen.
"Little star, wherever you are, please come and help," Laura called softly.

She went to bed and lay awake hoping for a very long time, but nothing happened.

In the middle of the night, Laura woke up. Her room was filled with a magical glow.

"I knew you'd come," Laura cried, as her star glittered in front of her. "I knew you'd help me if you could."

Laura felt full of hope. She got up and started to repair the kite. She glued strong paper over the rip. She drew teeth to make the kite look brave and bold. And all the time the star shone down, showering silvery light all around her.

At last the kite was finished. It looked brave and it looked bold. "But will it be brave and bold enough to reach the treetops?" Laura wondered.

Suddenly the star spun up above her and a sprinkle of stardust sparkled down on to the kite. It seemed as if the kite had a magical glow of its own.

"Thank you, star," whispered Laura. "This will be our secret. I can't wait to see Tommy's face when our little kite flies tomorrow."

The star twisted and twirled, as if it was dancing for her. Then it whirled away into the darkness.

"Goodnight, star," Laura called, as she watched it go.

"I've mended our kite," Laura said the next morning. "Let's take it to the park again."

"Joe and his friends will still bully us," Tommy said sadly. "It's still only a poor paper kite."

"Not any more," said Laura, with a smile. "It has a secret magic now. It's a very special kite."

Tommy didn't look too sure. "I can't see how it's special," he frowned.

"It's like the stars," Laura told him. "You can't see how magical they are during the day, but they're still there."

"I suppose so," said Tommy.

Joe and his friends were already at the park when Laura and Tommy arrived.

"It's the rubbish kite!" they jeered. "Haven't you put that in the bin yet?"

"Our kite is special," said Tommy, as loud as he dared.

Laura hugged him. "Remember what I said about believing in something, and then wishing for it? Try to believe in our kite now. And wish really, really hard."

"All right," Tommy nodded. "I'll try."

As Tommy watched, Laura began to run. She ran faster and faster. "Be brave, little kite – and be bold," she whispered.

The kite began to fly higher and higher. Joe and his friends stopped shouting and jeering. They just stood staring, with their mouths wide open.

"It's really flying," cried Laura. "See what it does for you, Tommy!"

Tommy took the kite from Laura. It soared above the treetops. It soared above the other kites.

"It wants to go even higher!" Tommy shouted to Laura. "It's pulling tighter on the string. I can't hold it much longer."

"Then maybe you should let it go," Laura said. "Maybe a kite as special as this one needs to be free."

Tommy let go.
The kite twisted and twirled, as if it was dancing for him. Then it whirled through the windy sky until it was just a tiny dot in the distance.
"Look," Tommy laughed. "My wish has come true. It's flying as high as the stars."
Laura smiled. "Fly all the way to my magic star," she whispered. "And say a special thank you from me."